PLANET AUT

Meet the alien friends...

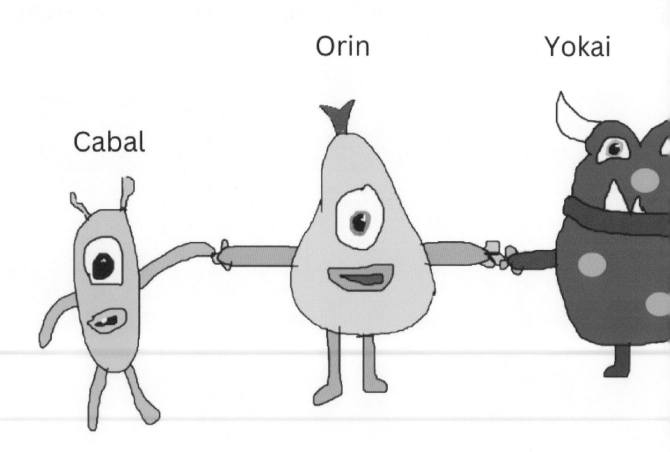

Cabal

Orin

Yokai

Rod

Oola

BEEP BEEP screamed the alarm clock. It was Yokai's least favorite time of the day, time to go to school.

"I'm so sick, I can't go to school! Also, I need to finish my artwork." whimpered Yokai.

BEEP BEEP

"Yokai, I know you don't enjoy it but all of us aliens need to go to school to help us learn and develop" said mom.

So, off he went to school...

First period, Yokai was sitting waiting patiently
for Miss Nommo to arrive to teach English class.

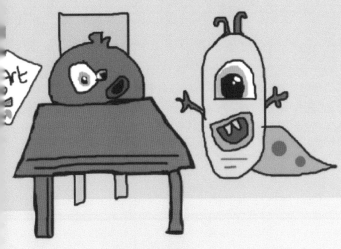

"Hi everyone, Miss Nommo
is sick, so I will be taking
today's class! Let's finish
our science project!" said
the new teacher.
Everyone cheered.

Everyone looked happy, except Yokai.
Yokai struggled with unexpected
changes to his routine.

Yokai began to flap his hands. Yokai did this
to help him to relax when he felt upset.

Yokai wished the lesson
would have just gone
ahead as planned.

"Why am I not like all of the other aliens?"
Yokai thought to himself.

At recess, everybody was screaming and shouting which hurt Yokai's ears.

AHH!

"Come play with us, Yokai!" offered Rod. Even though Yokai heard Rod trying to be kind, he didn't even look at him. Yokai ran away.

Rod was upset because he thought Yokai was being rude.

Yokai didn't mean to be rude. Yokai preferred to play alone with his trains. He wanted peace and quiet.

Yokai wished people would give him space and respect his wishes.
Yokai started rocking back and forth to help soothe himself.

"Why am I not like all of the other aliens?" Yokai thought to himself.

Math class is Yokai's favorite. He loves learning about addition.

However, Yokai found it very difficult to stay focused, especially because there are birds chirping outside.

The birds didn't seem to bother anyone else.

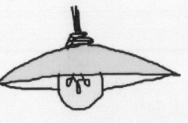

$+ 8 = 9$

This upset Mr Draco when Yokai lost focus.

"Yokai, concentrate! Pull yourself together!" shouted Mr Draco. Yokai was confused. He looked at his body, he wasn't broken. How could he pull himself together if he was already in one piece?

Yokai wished that he found easy to focus and pay attention.

"Why am I not like all of the other aliens?" Yokai thought to himself.

Yokai ate his usual lunch of chicken and rice.
He doesn't enjoy food with too much flavor.

"Hey Yokai, what's up?" Asked Rod.
Yokai looked up, "just the light" replied Yokai.
Everyone laughed. This made Yokai feel
confused and sad.

Yokai finished
organizing his lunch
box just how he liked
it, then he went
outside for recess.

Yokai was happily playing when all of a sudden he heard screaming.

Yokai's classmate, Orin, was on the floor and water was coming out of his eyes.

Yokai didn't know what to do. Everyone ran over to help.

Yokai wished could understand how Orin was feeling and that he knew how to help her feel better.

"Why am I not like all of the other aliens?" Yokai thought to himself.

All of a sudden, Yokai threw himself on the floor. He cried and screamed so loudly that even the aliens from the other planets could hear him.

HUH?

Everyone was confused.

What was going on?

Yokai's parents came to help Yokai to regulate his emotions.

The Principal, called Yokai's parents to his office to discuss how the school could be better at supporting Yokai with his social-emotional learning.

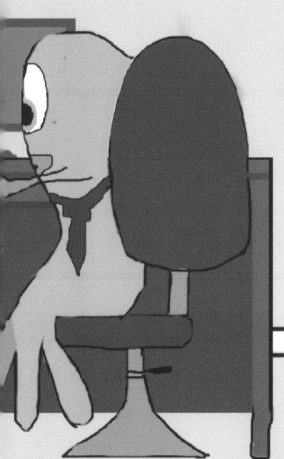

Mom wanted to explain something to the Principal. "Yokai has autism. Sometimes, everything gets overwhelming for him" explained Mom.

"Having autism means that Yokai's brain works in a different way" she said.

Mom continued to explain...

"Yokai can be sensitive to loud noises, bright lights, touching and strong smells.

It can be difficult to communicate, interact and understand emotions.

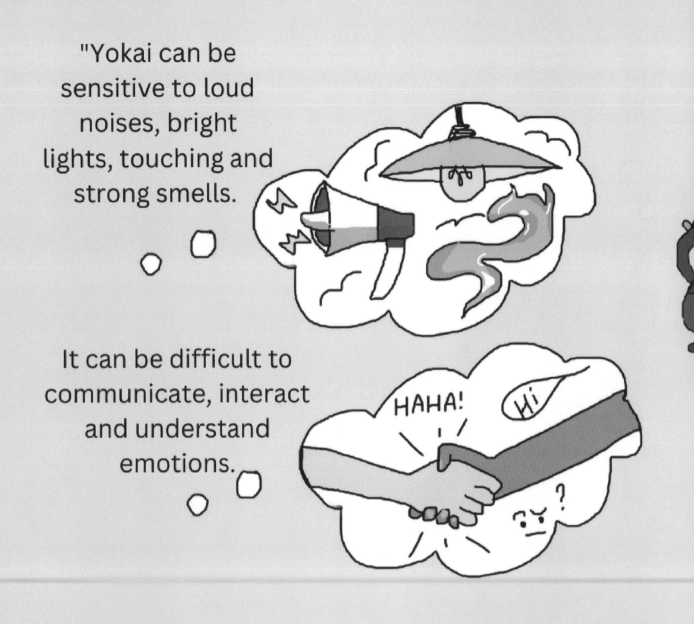

"However, Yokai has many talents that most other aliens do not have.

He is motivated, intelligent, and great at math.

$$1000 \times 1000 = 1,000,000$$

He is an amazing artist.

He has a fine eye for detail, and is passionate about trains. Yokai loves to problem-solve."

"Yokai feels all the same emotions all the other aliens feel. He just shows them and understands them in a different way."

"All aliens should support each other..."

Yokai, can you show us your train?

"Being different is not a bad thing. After all, all of us aliens are different in our own way."

"We can all help by being kind, understanding and **inclusive.**"

"We are all different and unique and that is what makes Planet Earth such a cool place" said Mom finally.

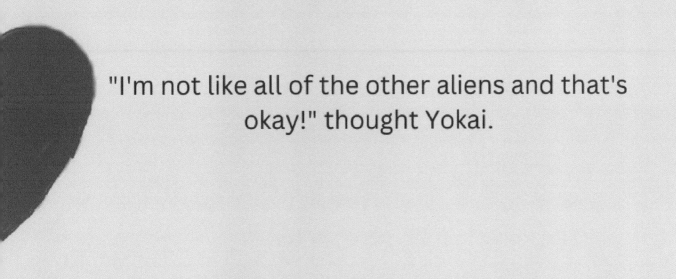

"I'm not like all of the other aliens and that's okay!" thought Yokai.

Yokai was so tired, that felt like the longest day ever!

"I'm proud of you, Yokai. Now your teachers and classmates understand you better, they will know how to support you," Dad said joyfully.

WHAT IS AUTISM?

Everyone is different. Some differences are easy to see.

Some differences you can't see, like autism. Autism affects the brain.

People with autism express themselves differently. Some speak a lot, others not at all.

Some people with autism can find it difficult to understand others' emotions...

..and expressing their own emotions. Sometimes they display behaviors that are surpring.

They can have intense fears we may find difficult to understand.

They can have intense interests that we may find surpring.

People with autism deserve to be loved and respected just like everyone else.

Some people with autism easily learn complicated things. Having autism doesn't prevent them from living a beautiful life.

Inclusion: Respecting and accepting other people's differences. Making everyone feel welcomed and part of the group, with a sense of belonging.

Printed in Great Britain
by Amazon